The Mystery of the Dog with 1000 Disguises

From the files of Police Dog 99 . . .

← expensive
chocolate bone

Keith Brumpton

ORCHARD BOOKS

ORCHARD BOOKS
96 Leonard Street, London EC2A 4RH
Orchard Books Australia
14 Mars Road, Lane Cove, NSW 2066
ISBN 1 85213 448 8 (hardback)
ISBN 1 85213 665 0 (paperback)
First published in Great Britain 1993
First paperback publication 1994
© Keith Brumpton 1993
The right of Keith Brumpton to be identified as the author of
this work has been asserted by him in accordance with the
Copyright, Designs and Patents Act, 1988.
A CIP catalogue record for this book is available from
the British Library.
Printed in Great Britain

Contents

Open the book and let's catch a crook!

ON THE TRAIL OF
THE DOG WITH 1000 DISGUISES

Welcome once more to Whistlebridge Police Station where another crime is waiting to be solved. My name is Rusty Barker, Police Dog 99, and on this case I'll be working as usual with my faithful assistant, Police Constable Andy Constable.

Anyway, time is too short for idle yaps, so settle back and enjoy the mysterious case of the dog with 1000 disguises.

Chapter One

Odeon III – the argument

It was a wet and windy night in Whistle-bridge. Inside Andy's house the curtains were drawn and the gas fire was on. The *Radio Times* was open at just the right page.

Upstairs I could hear the sound of Andy getting ready. He was going to the pictures with his girlfriend, W.P.C. Sally Swancourt. Probably to see some awful film with lots of romance and kissing. Yuk! They never went to see anything good like *Rottweiler II*, or *Lassie Meets the Alien*.

Not that I was worried. It was our night off and as a special treat Andy had let me into the front lounge for a little snooze on the rug.

I'd already chewed my tennis ball and nibbled my bone, so all in all I was feeling about as contented as a Great Dane with its teeth in a tramp's bottom.

Just then the phone went. What d'you mean, "Where did it go?" I mean it rang. It went "brrr". It was Sally for Andy. (I never get many calls, which is probably just as well 'cos holding the receiver in your mouth is pretty tricky.)

Andy was talking to Sally and trying to finish getting dressed at the same time. It was a horrible sight. He seemed to be getting a bit annoyed.

"What d'you mean you can't go?!?"

"I've got a karate lesson. It's very important. I really can't afford to miss it. We can go to the pictures another time."

"But this is the last night the film's on," spluttered Andy. "And my mum says it's really good."

"Why not take Rusty then?" replied Sally.

(Me and Sally always got on really well).

Andy didn't seem too happy with this suggestion though. He said he'd see Sally around and put down the phone. I hadn't seen him so angry since I accidentally spilt Pedigree

Chum over his Police Examinations certificate.

Anyway, bang went my quiet evening in. I had to go to the pictures to keep Andy company. He kept telling me how good this film *The Big Romance* was going to be, but in the end I managed to talk him into going to the Odeon III instead.

← grumpy look

He seemed to enjoy the film, but he was very quiet on the way home.

What would happen to him and Sally? Would they get back together again, or was this really the end?

Chapter Two
Mutt in the middle

Whistlebridge Police Station was a hive of activity. Everyone was looking lively in case they bumped into Sergeant Brisket. Sergeant Brisket was so strict he sometimes used to tell himself off!

The Sarge practising in front of a mirror

Call that a telling off, Sergeant Brisket ??? I've seen tougher looking hamsters !!!

Andy was in the corridor when Sally appeared next to him. They weren't speaking and they both turned as red as a bottle of ketchup.

"Rusty, can you tell Constable Constable I'm not talking to him until he apologises?"

I turned around and looked at Andy, but there was no sign of an apology.

I turned and looked at Sally. She gave me a pat on the head and walked off. Andy opened his mouth but said nothing.

What a start to the day!

Chapter Three
A difficult mission!

Sergeant Brisket's temper was as short as the short bit in a piece of shortbread. He had just been given the latest crime figures for Whistlebridge and they didn't make good reading.

"It's a disgrace!" he snorted, while striding down the corridor. "We've got too many coppers who couldn't catch a cold never mind a criminal. Heads will have to roll!" Just then he turned the corner and saw Andy blowing his nose.

"Constable Constable!" he bellowed, "I want to see you and the mutt in my office."

19

Talk about Prince Charming!

Sergeant Brisket's office was as neat as a whippet's whiskers. Not a thing was out of place. You could even see your own reflection in the wastepaper bin.

polished door handles

GLEAM

book of police rules

There was even a sign asking people not to put litter in the waste-paper bin!

Our superior thrust a very thick bundle of papers towards us.

"... This is the file on Billy the Peke. Also known as Monty the Mongrel, Fifi the Labrador, and so on. As you'll see, he's a master of disguise. One of the most unpleasant villains operating on our patch. We suspect that recently he's committed a number of crimes in the Batterfish Park area.

"His method is very cunning. He disguises

himself as some poor helpless stray dog, and then waits to be adopted by someone. Usually a lonely old pensioner. Once he's inside their home he carries out his crimes – obtaining bones under false pretences, stealing their valuables and so on."

"Exactly. I want you and the fleabag here to investigate."

Fleabag! The cheek of it! I've only got about five fleas and I'm on very good terms with them all.

"... I warn you," continued the Sarge, "if you don't come up with some answers on this case I shall be recommending you both for transfer to another station!"

Andy's face went as white as a bottle of milk in a blizzard. What a disaster it would be if we were transferred!

1. He might never see Sally again!
2. His mum would have to send his sandwiches through the post!!

3. Think of the bones I would have to leave behind in the garden!!!

The Sarge handed over the notes on the case and told us we had forty-eight hours. Forty-eight hours! Even Sherlock Bones would have needed more time than that.

Chapter Four

Billy the Peke: the lowdown

We don't think this is his own handbag.

There had been three robberies that we knew of for certain. And all in the same area – Batterfish Park.

Batterfish Park

Andy handed me half a Twix and we looked through the file together.

Case number one

Mrs Betty Brittlebottom, aged seventy.

A popular figure in Whistlebridge. She coaches two basketball teams, eats only cheese and biscuits, and enjoys Church discos.

Awoke to find that someone had swiped her jewellery, two boxes of toffees, and her skateboard. There was no one in the house at the time except for her deaf budgie, Brendan, and a stray dog she'd found earlier in the week. The stray dog disappeared soon after.

"Nothing there to help us," said Andy, turning to the next case and eating a pickled onion sandwich his mum had packed.

chomp

I hate pickled onions.

Case number two

Mr Tommy Dodgem, aged eighty. Retired boxer.

punch bag

Old Tommy still liked to work out...

But he was a bit past it !!!

Had his medals stolen, and six packets of biscuits. No witnesses except for a stray dog he'd met earlier that week.

There seemed to be a pattern emerging, but Andy couldn't see it. The last pattern he'd seen was a jumper his auntie had knitted for him.

Very nice, auntie.

"Read the last one," I yapped, "and let's see if the facts fit."

Case number three
Mr Jimmy Singh, aged seventy-one.

Reported losing a valuable diamond, two samosas and a quarter of a pound of best mince. He was alone at the time except for his four-year-old granddaughter and their new pet, a Labrador called Gus. They'd found Gus the week before, wandering in the park.

"Could it have been the granddaughter?" asked Andy. Sometimes he was about as bright as a foggy day in Frickley.

"These crimes are all the work of Billy the

Peke," I growled. "And it's quite clear how he operates."

"It is?"

"Woof. Yes. It's just like the Sarge said. He disguises himself as a stray dog and then hangs around the park waiting to be taken home. Now we have to think of a way of catching him out before he steals from anyone else and before we get put on the transfer list."

Andy finished the last of his pickled onion sandwiches and a worried look came over his face.

"D'you think we can do it, Rusty? I don't want to be transferred."

I gave his hand a friendly lick and we headed home.

Chapter Five
Down to work

All next morning I paced the backyard trying to think of a way to outsmart Billy the Peke.

Andy didn't. He'd caught cold. He was missing Sally. And his mum had forgotten to send the sandwiches.

Now, if you'll forgive me, I've got some thinking to do.

Chapter Six

An old burger gives inspiration

The answer came to me, late in the afternoon, as Andy and I were out walking down the high street.

I stopped to sniff an old quarter-pounder and found myself looking in the window of a second-hand clothes shop.

I looked at the clothes and I looked at Andy and something clicked. (No, not just Andy's knees.)

That evening at Andy's we rehearsed everything. At first Andy wasn't very keen – you'll probably see why in a moment.

"You're sure there's no other way?" he asked, with a pleading look in his eyes. I shook my head and Andy went upstairs to get changed.

When he returned you would hardly have recognised him. In fact that was the general idea. We'd bought some clothes from the second-hand clothes shop, and used some make-up we found at Andy's mum's. Poor Andy didn't look a day under seventy.

I shook my head. "Certainly not. If we're to convince Billy the Peke that you're a helpless old pensioner we'll have to make sure you look the part."

"But I've got all the clothes on."

"Woof. But we still need to work on your movement. You've got to think like an old-aged pensioner and act like one."

It was going to be a long evening.

long evening

short evening

Chapter Seven
Andy the O.A.P.

I got up early the next morning, chased a few tennis balls around, had a quick splash in a puddle, and got Andy out of bed.

By nine o'clock he was dressed in his disguise and we were on our way to the shops to buy some cream crackers. This would be the first test of Andy's outfit. Fortunately no one in the shop seemed to recognise him.

On the pavement he was jostled by a couple of angry shoppers.

Two old women stopped for a chat. "See you at the pop-in centre tonight. There's old-time dancing ..."

Things were going really well when Andy almost gave the whole game away by running for the bus.

"You want to take it easy, old lad," smiled the bus driver. "You might overheat your longjohns running at that speed."

Andy sat down looking very embarrassed.

We spent most of the morning in Batterfish Park hoping that Billy the Peke would show up and fall into our trap. But though we saw dogs of every shape and size, none of them came up to us, and lunch-time arrived with no sign of the criminal.

Andy decided to go to the café over the road for a cup of tea. Because we were "under cover" I said I'd stay in the park and keep my eyes peeled. As Andy was crossing the road a young policewoman suddenly appeared at his side. It was Sally!

For an awful moment it looked as if our plan was going to be ruined. But fortunately even Sally didn't recognise Andy through his disguise. In fact, she offered to help him cross the road.

You want to watch it, love. It's very busy here. Here, give me your arm.

Andy pulled his scarf up tight.

" ... That's right. You keep yourself warm. There's a chill in that wind today. I'm just off-duty now. Looking for my boyfriend ... He's a policeman as well. We had a bit of an argument. I'm trying to find him to patch things up, but he seems to have vanished off the face of the earth!"

Andy was just about to take off his disguise when a small black dog appeared next to him, its tail wagging, and looking very friendly.

"... Looks like you've found a friend," smiled Sally, and headed off up the road.

Andy bent down to stroke the little black mongrel.

I sniffed the air and looked closely at the newly arrived pooch. Could this be Billy the Peke up to his old tricks?

I wonder...

Chapter Eight
Is it, or isn't it?

Try as he might, Andy couldn't shake off the little black dog. You'd think someone had stuck it to his trouser leg with super-glue.

I was now very suspicious. I hoped that Andy would have the good sense to head back home and see if the dog followed, but no such luck. He was feeling hot and tired beneath his overcoat and false moustache and decided that it was time to ask a few questions.

He took off his coat and was just reaching into his pocket for his police I.D. card when the mystery mongrel got wind that something was up and scarpered as fast as its four legs would carry it.

Andy set off in pursuit,

trod on his scarf,

and landed up in a Parks Department wheelbarrow, heading at speed towards the bowling green ...

The captain of the Ladies Bowls Team shouted as Andy sped past.

The mystery black dog was heading hot-paw for the boating lake, with me on its heels. I wish my friend Ted the greyhound had been there. This mutt was turbo-charged!

Andy and his barrow eventually came to a halt in a flower-bed and he looked around to see where I'd got to. Between us we'd somehow managed to corner the suspect down by the boat shed. There was no escape now, unless he swam for it!

Chapter Nine
Wet, wet, wet

"Splash!"

There's nothing as desperate as a desperate villain (unless you count Mrs Constable's rock cakes; they're pretty desperate).

The black dog was doggy-paddling to the other side of the lake.

"After him!" shouted Andy.

"What d'you mean, you can't swim? ALL dogs can swim."

"Not me. What about you?"

Andy shook his head. "Not without my water-wings. And I haven't got them here."

The black dog had almost reached the middle of the lake.

"Then we'll have to take a boat," I yapped, and leaped into the nearest paddle-boat. Andy followed slowly. He didn't like the water very much. He wouldn't even run the bath too deep in case he slipped on his soap.

"Ship away!" Andy began paddling as fast as he could while I barked encouragement. Slowly but surely we began to gain on the dark-haired mongrel, though Andy was already beginning to tire.

You couldn't exactly say that he was the Arnie Schwarzenegger type; in fact I've seen more muscles on a peanut. But there's one thing I like about Andy – he's determined!

Gradually we began to gain on the paddling pooch.

Ten metres ... Five ... Three ... Two ...

"Stop right there!" he shouted, after we'd drawn alongside our suspect. "You are not obliged to say anything, but anything you do say can, er, ... Anyway, you're under arrest, Billy."

But was it Billy?

The black mongrel was too tired even to reply. We'd reached the other side of the lake and we were all worn out.

weary look

Chapter Ten
Let's take a peek at Billy the Peke

"OK, Copper, you've got me rumbled," sniffed Billy, taking off his disguise. "That was a smart trick disguising yourself like that. Beat me at my own game."

Andy looked proudly across and gave me a friendly wink. I didn't mind him getting the credit now and then. After all, we're a team, and I like to see my assistant get some reward for all his hard work. Also I knew there'd be a treat that evening – a bar of chocolate, or maybe even a new squeaky toy. I certainly wasn't complaining.

Back at the station we were busy filling out our report when Andy's mum phoned. She wanted to know what Andy wanted in his sandwiches next day. Andy didn't normally like his mum calling the station because he said it didn't look very professional, but tonight he was in a good mood and ordered up some corned beef and onion (my favourites too, except for the onion).

Sergeant Brisket couldn't quite believe that we'd cracked the case. He congratulated Andy and even tried to give me a pat on the bonce.

Deep down inside he was probably feeling annoyed because now he wouldn't be able to recommend us for a transfer. He said we'd done well for beginners and to try and keep up the good work.

Billy the Peke was under lock and key in the police cells, and eventually told us where we

could find the stolen goods (except for the quarter of a pound of Mr Singh's mince, which he'd long since eaten).

So, everything had turned out OK in the end. Except for what?

Oh, yes, you want to know about Andy and Sally.

Chapter Eleven
Time to get pally with Sally

I waited outside while Andy got the car from the garage. As usual, this took ages, because he isn't a very good driver. We were the only car on the road that used to be overtaken by pedestrians!

Sally was very pleased to see us, especially when Andy said he was sorry for having been so bad-tempered, and when he told the story of how we'd managed to catch Billy the Peke.

"Why don't we go to the pictures tonight?" suggested Sally after a while. "Sort of a celebration."

Andy looked really pleased. "Great idea."

"Just the three of us."

"THREE?"

"Yeah. And to make sure there's no arguments we'll let Rusty choose the film."

Important message from the
Crimewatch UK team

Since this book was printed we are sorry to have to inform you that Billy the Peke has escaped from police custody while disguised as an elderly collie. He may be in *your* neighbourhood.

Please assist the police by keeping your eyes open for any suspicious-looking dogs, particularly any answering the following descriptions:

Trevor the Collie
Monty the Mongrel
Charlie the Spaniel

Thank you for your help.

Also by Keith Brumpton:
  A Dinosaur's Book of Dinosaurs
  Ig and Tig's Trip to Earth
  Dinosaur World Cup
  Police Dog 99 Investigates: The Mystery of
    the Missing Moggie

Also by Rusty:
  A User's Guide to Trees in Whistlebridge

Really the end